The last magic adventure had gone wrong.
Floppy had been left behind. A giant bird had flown
off with him. This was because a horrid genie had
escaped from a bottle.

"And it was all my fault," said Biff.

"We've got to rescue Floppy," said Chip.
"We must go back into the adventure."

"But we can't make the key glow," said Biff.

"I know," said Chip, "but we must try. We have
to find a way to get the genie back in the bottle."

Biff and Chip looked at the magic key.

"Oh, if only it would glow," said Biff.

Then the magic key did begin to glow. The magic took the children back into the last adventure.

The magic took them to an island. Biff had
been there before. It was the island where the
giant bird had flown away with Floppy. Kamar
was still there. He was with his father, Hassan.

Hassan and Kamar were mending their boat.
Kamar ran to meet them.

"You have come back!" he said to Biff.
"Where have you been?"

"You wouldn't believe it," said Biff, "even if we
told you."

"This is my brother, Chip," said Biff. "We have come back to rescue Floppy."

Kamar shook his head.

"That will be very dangerous," he said. "The giant bird took him up to the top of that mountain."

"I know," said Biff, "and that's where we're
going. We must get up there as fast as we can."

"Stop!" shouted Kamar. "Don't go! Have you
forgotten about the evil genie?"

"We'll worry about him later," said Chip.

Biff and Chip went as fast as they could, but
it was hard work. They had to climb over big
rocks. At last they came to the mountain.
Biff was tired. She sat on a rock for a rest.

The mountain looked steep and rocky.

"How can we climb up?" asked Biff.

Then Chip found a dried up stream.

"Come on," called Chip. "This gully looks an easy way up."

Biff and Chip began to climb up the gully. Suddenly there was a loud noise and a terrible smell. It was the evil genie. He was standing at the top of the gully.

"Ha! I can soon get rid of you," he shouted.

The genie clapped his hands. Water began to gush down the gully. Biff and Chip had no time to climb out. The water rushed towards them.

"Quickly, Biff! Climb on to this rock and hang on," shouted Chip.

Biff and Chip hung on to the rock. The water roared past them. Biff and Chip were frightened.

"What are we going to do?" shouted Biff.

"I don't know," called Chip. "It's too far to jump to safety."

Then they saw Kamar. He had followed them to the mountain.

"Hang on!" he shouted. "I'll soon have you safe." He threw a rope across the gully. It caught on a branch on the other side.

Biff and Chip climbed to safety on the rope.

"We are so pleased to see you!" said Biff.
"I thought we'd never get off that rock."

"The evil genie did this," said Chip.

"It's a good job I came when I did,"
said Kamar. "I came to help you rescue Floppy."

They began to climb the mountain again. Biff and Chip were pleased that Kamar had come to help them. The giant bird was flying high above them.

"What have you done with Floppy?" yelled Biff crossly.

It took them a long time to get to the top of the mountain. At last they reached the nest of the giant bird.

"Ugh!" said Chip. "Look at all these bones. I hope the bird hasn't eaten Floppy!"

"Floppy," called Biff, "where are you?"

Then they saw Floppy. He was fast asleep and he had a contented look on his face. In front of him was a pile of bones.

"Oh Floppy!" said Biff. "Wake up!"
Floppy woke up and wagged his tail.

"We must get back quickly," said Kamar.
"The evil genie may use his powers again."

"I'm glad we're going," thought Floppy, "but
I'm sorry I can't take *all* the lovely bones."
They went down the mountain as fast as they
could.

Then they saw Hassan. He had come to look
for them.

"I am so glad I have found you," he said.
"I have been worried about you."

"We are all safe," said Kamar, "and we have
rescued Floppy."

Hassan was worried. He looked at Kamar.

"The genie may use his powers again. We must get away from the island as quickly as we can," he said.

They began to load things into the boat.

Chip looked at the old chest on the beach.
It had been washed up in a storm.

"I don't know what's inside it," said Hassan.
"It could be treasure."

"Why don't you open it?" asked Chip.

"I don't have a key," said Hassan.

Chip had an idea.

"Lend me the magic key, Biff," he said.

He put the key in the lock and turned it. The lid of the chest sprang open. Everyone looked in the chest, but it was completely empty.

Suddenly there was a crackling sound and a terrible smell of old burnt socks. The evil genie appeared!

"Ha!" he shouted. "You have escaped my powers too many times. Now I will deal with you once and for all."

Chip thought of a way to trick the genie.
Quickly he shut the lid of the chest.

"Why did you shut that chest?" asked the genie.
"What is inside it?"

"Er... it's something very valuable," said Chip.

"Is it treasure?" asked the genie.

"It's a lot more valuable than treasure,"
said Chip.
The genie looked in the chest.

"There's nothing valuable in here," he shouted.

"Oh, but there is," said Chip. "You're just not
looking hard enough."
The genie bent inside the chest to look.

Suddenly Chip pushed the genie into the chest and slammed down the lid. Then he locked it with the magic key.

"How dare you!" shouted the genie. "You will pay for this when I get out."

"But you can't get out," called Chip.

"Oh yes I can," shouted the genie. "I can't get out of bottles, but it's easy to get out of a chest."

"But you're locked in," said Chip. "We don't believe you can get out."

"I'll use my powers," said the genie.

The genie made himself thin and started to slip through the keyhole. Chip held the bottle over the keyhole. And the genie slid into it.

"He fell for my trick," said Chip. "I thought he would."

Hassan and Kamar shook Chip's hand.

"That was brilliant, Chip!" said Kamar.
"The genie is safely in the bottle. Now we can all
go home."

"I'm glad it was all right in the end," said Biff.
"And I'm glad Floppy is safe."

The magic key began to glow. It was time to go.

"I bet Floppy hated this adventure," said Chip. Floppy looked at them both.

"I don't know," he thought. "I quite enjoyed it, really."

The magic took them home. Kipper ran into
Biff's room.

"Hooray! You rescued Floppy!" he said.
"What happened to the evil genie?"

"We put him back in the bottle," said Chip.

The children looked at the little chest.

"I'm glad the bottle didn't come back from the adventure," said Kipper.

Biff tried to lift the lid of the chest, but it wouldn't open.

"And now the key won't fit," she laughed.